Parents and Caregivers,

Stone Arch Readers are designed to provide enjoyable reading experiences, as well as opportunities to develop vocabulary, literacy skills, and comprehension. Here are a few ways to support your beginning reader:

- Talk with your child about the ideas addressed in the story.

- Discuss each illustration, mentioning the characters, where they are, and what they are doing.

- Read with expression, pointing to each word You may want to read the whole story through and then revisit parts of the story to ensure that the meanings of words or phrases are understood.

- Talk about why the character did what he or she did and what your child would do in that situation.

- Help your child connect with characters and events in the story.

Remember, reading with your child should be fun, not forced. Each moment spent reading with your child is a priceless investment in his or her literacy life.

Gail Saunders-Smith, Ph.D.

STONE ARCH **READERS**

are published by Stone Arch Books, a Capstone Imprint
151 Good Counsel Drive, P.O. Box 669
Mankato, Minnesota 56002
www.capstonepub.com

Library of Congress Cataloging-in-Publication data
is available on the Library of Congress website.
ISBN: 978-1-4342-2049-3 (library binding)
ISBN: 978-1-4342-2793-5 (paperback)

Summary: The Pet Club is going camping, and Andy is worried
about sleeping in the tent all by himself.

Reading Consultants:
Gail Saunders-Smith, Ph.D.
Melinda Melton Crow, M.Ed.
Laurie K. Holland, Media Specialist

Art Director: Kay Fraser
Designer: Emily Harris
Production Specialist: Michelle Biedscheid

The NOISY Night

A PET CLUB STORY

by Gwendolyn Hooks

illustrated by Mike Byrne

STONE ARCH BOOKS
a capstone imprint

Meet
the
PET CLUB!

Lucy, Jake, Kayla, and Andy are best friends. Lucy has a rat named Ajax. Jake has a dog named Buddy.

Kayla

Andy

Daisy

Nibbles

Kayla has a cat named Daisy.
Andy has a fish named Nibbles.
Together, they are the Pet Club!

The Pet Club is going camping.

Andy packs the sleeping bags. Kayla packs the pillows. Jake packs the food. Lucy packs the flashlight.

"Grab your pets!" Andy says.

"Let's go," Andy's mom says.

It's a long drive to the campsite.
Everyone is excited.

Everyone helps set up camp.

"It's hot," Kayla says.

"I'm ready to swim," Jake says.

After swimming, it is dark out.
Everyone is hungry.

They roast hot dogs over the fire.

Lucy tells a scary story.

Andy is scared. He holds on tight
to Nibbles.

"I'm still hungry," Jake says.

"So am I," Lucy says.

Jake roasts marshmallows.
Kayla shares cupcakes. Andy
doesn't feel like eating.

"Time for bed," Andy's mom says.

"Does anyone want to share my tent?" Andy asks.

"My tent is just the right size for me and Buddy," says Jake.

"Kayla and I are sharing a tent," says Lucy.

Andy turns on his flashlight.
He zips his tent. He checks on
Nibbles.

He crawls into his sleeping bag.

The night is too quiet.

Andy feels alone and scared.

Andy hears some scratches
outside his tent.

Then he hears a whisper.

"Andy, let me in."

Andy turns on his flashlight.
He opens his tent.

Jake and Buddy are standing
outside.

"What are you doing here?"
Andy asks.

"I think Buddy is scared,"
Jake says.

"Just Buddy?" Andy asks.

"Maybe I'm a little scared, too," Jake says.

Andy is not scared anymore.
Neither is Jake.

Andy, Nibbles, Jake, and Buddy
fall fast asleep.

STORY WORDS

flashlight   marshmallows   roast

campsite   scared   tent

Total Word Count: 286

Join the Pet Club today!

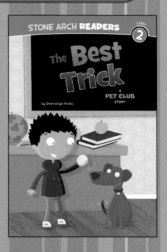

So did Fred.